# Crispin
## The Pig Who Had It All

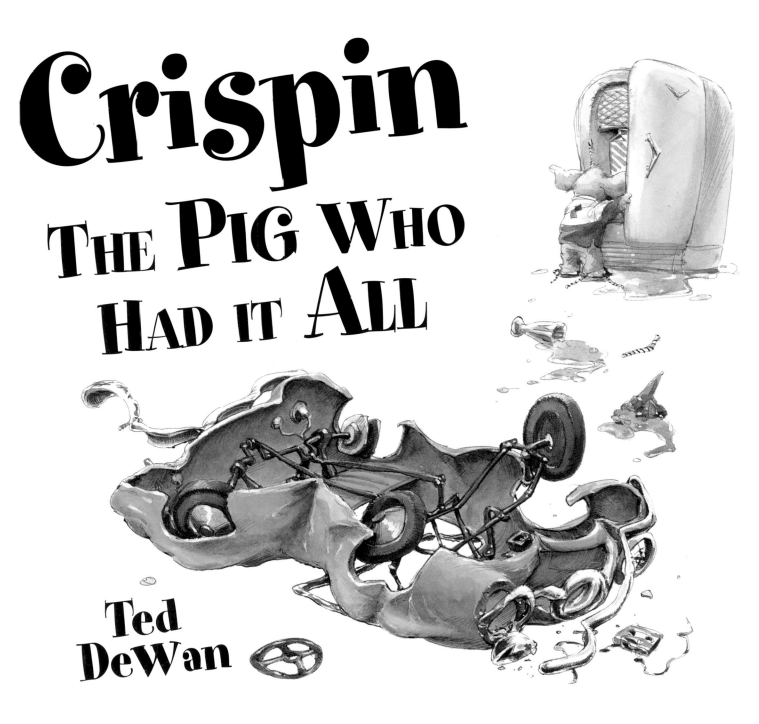

Ted
DeWan

A Doubleday Book for Young Readers

*This book is dedicated to*
*Scott,*
*Chris,*
*Tim,*
*and, of course,*
*Crispin,*
*who helped me put the bits together*

A Doubleday Book for Young Readers

Published by
Random House Children's Books
a division of
Random House, Inc.
1540 Broadway
New York, New York 10036

Doubleday is a registered trademark of
Random House, Inc.

First American Edition 2000
First published in Great Britain by Doubleday,
a division of Transworld Publishers, 2000

Visit us on the Web! www.randomhouse.com/kids
Educators and librarians, for a variety of teaching tools, visit us at
www.randomhouse.com/teachers

Library of Congress Cataloging-in-Publication Data

ISBN: 0-385-32540-1

Cataloging-in-Publication Data is available from the Library of Congress.

The text of this book is set in Bodoni Infant.

Manufactured in Singapore

October 2000

10 9 8 7 6 5 4 3 2 1

PLEASE NOTE THAT THE CRISPIN IN THIS BOOK IN NO WAY RESEMBLES ANY ACTUAL CRISPINS, LIVING OR DEAD

Crispin Tamworth was a pig who had it all.

And at Christmas, he got even more.

One Christmas, he got a  ZYBOX™ TEDDY-BOT.

But by Easter,
        he was bored with it . . . .

. . . and then it got broken.

The next Christmas, he got a
SPEEDPONY™ SHOCKJOCKEY.

But by Valentine's Day,
   he was bored with it . . .

. . . and then it got broken.

Last Christmas, he got a GIGA-PIGSTATION™ and all the latest computer games.

But by New Year's Day, he was already bored with it . . .

. . . and, as usual,  it got broken.

This Christmas, when he woke up early
to peek at his toys,
Crispin found an enormous box.

Master
Crispin,
In this box
you will find
the only thing
you do not have.
It's the very best
thing in the
whole wide world.
S

"Oh boy!"
squeaked Crispin.

He pulled the ribbon,
lifted the top of the box,
and peeped inside.

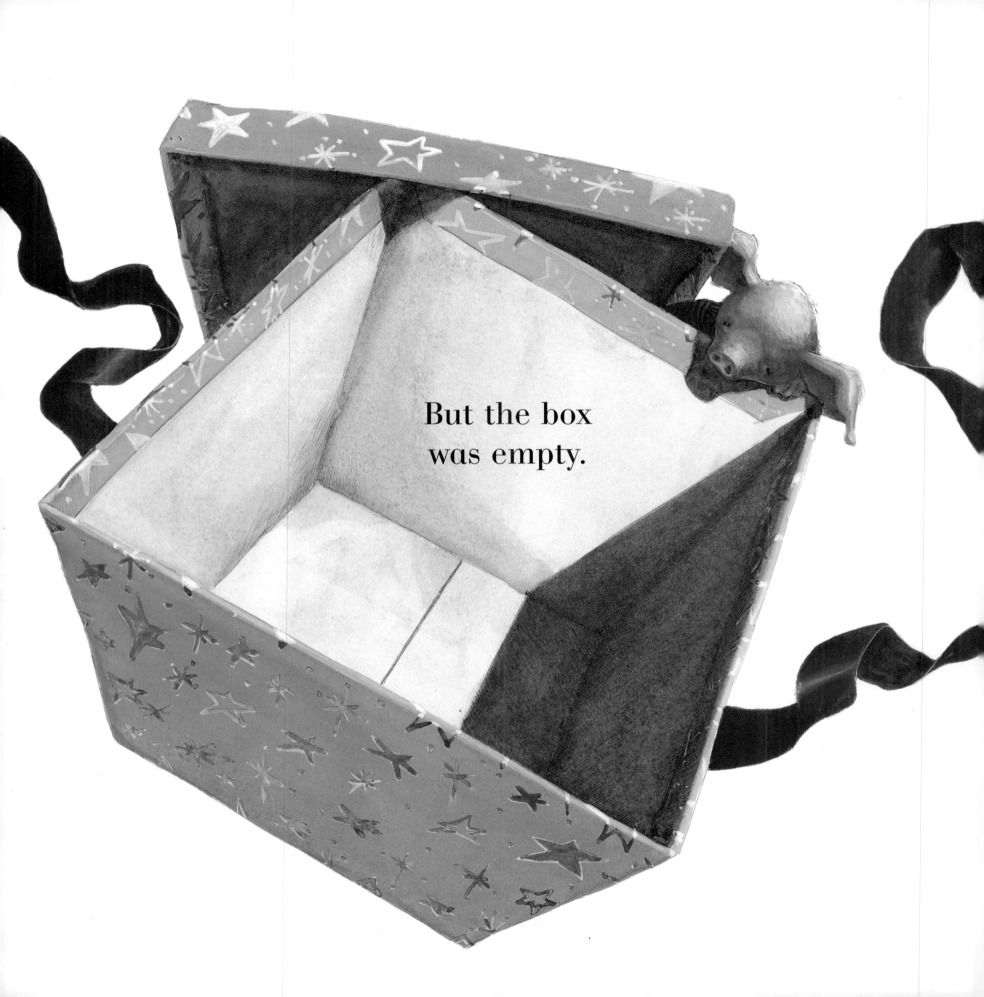

But the box
was empty.

There was nothing inside at all.

Crispin sat by the Christmas tree and cried.

"What's the matter, Crispin dear?" cooed Mrs. Tamworth.

"Santa gave me nothing for Christmas," snuffled Crispin.

"Weren't you a good pig this year?" grunted Mr. Tamworth.

"Oh, it must have been a mistake," said Mrs. Peck, the housekeeper. "I'm sure Santa didn't mean to make you sad."

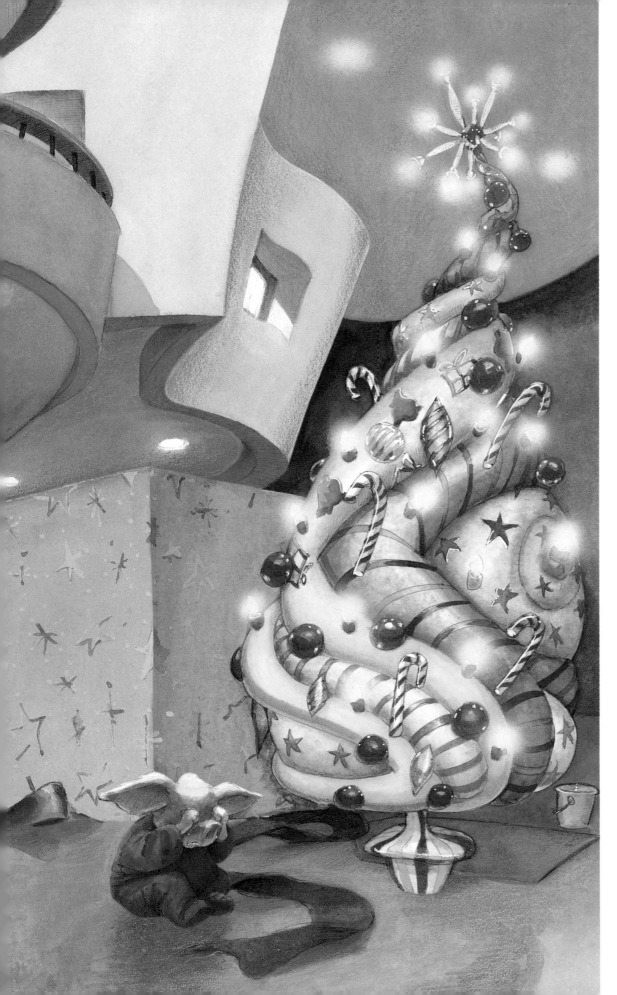

But Crispin
was very sad.

He shoved the box
out the front door.

Then he went
to his room and
stayed there all
Christmas morning.

He didn't even
come down
for his Christmas
dinner.

Crispin sat by his window
and watched as a rabbit and a raccoon
walked into his front yard.

"What a great box!"
said the rabbit.
"Come on, let's take it,"
said the raccoon.

But Crispin didn't want anyone else to take his box.

"Hmm, this is no fun," he said.

Soon Crispin was cold. So he went back inside.

The next day, Nick and Penny
crept back to play in Crispin's box.

"Hey, that's MINE," Crispin oinked. "Get out!"
"We're not wrecking anything," said Penny.
"We're playing Space Base."

"I don't see any Space Base," grunted Crispin.
"Look out, Penny!" screamed Nick. "ALIEN!"

"I'm not the alien, YOU'RE the alien," said Crispin.
"This is my property—now you GET OUT!"

"BZZZAP!" shouted Nick. "GOTCHA, ALIEN SCUM!"

"Ha! Missed me by a mile," squealed Crispin.

And so they
all played
Space Base
until sunset.

**O**n Saturday,
Mr. Tamworth gave
Crispin his pocket money.

"Aren't you going off to the
arcade today?" asked
Mr. Tamworth.

"Not today,"
said Crispin.

"Nick and Penny might come by."

Nick and Penny did come by, and they all played **STORE**,

**PIRATES,**

CASTLE,

and, of course,
their favorite . . .

SPACE BASE.

They played so long that Crispin was late for supper.

**T**hat night,
the weather changed.
It rained and rained.
All the snow melted.

So did
Crispin's box.

"My box is ruined,"
Crispin sobbed.
"Now my friends won't
come over anymore."

But, of course, his friends did come over.

"Look at all this stuff!" shouted Nick.
"Aw, it's all broken," said Crispin. "It's junk."

But his friends didn't think so.

They helped Crispin gather the broken bits of the Zybox™ Teddy-bot

and the SpeedPony™ ShockJockey

and the Giga-Pigstation™

and they all had a hopping good game of . . .

They played until way after suppertime,
and almost missed dessert.

One Friday after school,
Crispin brought his friends back to play.

"Hi, kids!" said Mrs. Peck. "Come in and
see our brand-new fridge. It's just arrived,
and it makes
ice cream!"

"Brilliant!" piped
Crispin's friends.

"Oh, Crispin," said Mrs. Peck, "the fridge deliveryman took away all that junk in your room. Now it's nice and tidy."

"JUNK!"
shouted Crispin.
"That wasn't
junk!

It was a store . . .
and a pirate ship . . .
and a castle . . .
and SPACE BASE . . .
and you threw it all away!"

"All my pals will go away.
There's nothing here to play with."


Crispin wept.

But right there in his own back garden
was the great big box
that the fridge came in.

Crispin went
and peeped inside
the empty box . . .

. . . and he saw
that it was full.